Timmy the Turd Burglar

JAMES CHRISTOPHER
ISBN: 9798869724984

This Book Belongs to:

_____

_____

_____

Color Test Chart

In a town quite absurd, a Turd Burglar roamed, Mischief and pranks, are the seeds he'd sown.

Toilet paper trails and soap on the floor, He'd chuckle and giggle, always wanting more.

The townsfolk grumbled, their patience thin, at Turd Burglar's antics and continuous grin .

No kindness in his heart, just a love for the jest, The town yearned for a change, a break from the unrest.

Soap suds spilled, creating
a slippery dance,
The Turd Burglar laughed, giving
mischief a chance.

Puddles of water where they shouldn't be, The townsfolk puzzled, "Who could it be?"

Mailboxes filled with confetti and glue, The town's frustration grew & grew.

As the town stirred, a mischievous spree, Turd Burglar's pranks flourished, wild and free.

Laughter erupted, but not all were pleased, The townsfolk yearned for the pranks to cease.

One moonlit night, a mysterious plan, The town decided to take a stand.

Sneaky whispers, a plot underway,
Turd Burglar, unsuspecting,
continued his play.

A bucket of glitter hung high in the air, Turd Burglar walked beneath, blissfully unaware.

Glitter rained down, a shimmering shower, Turd Burglar's laughter turned into a glower.

Covered in sparkles, the whole town cheered, Turd Burglar, once feared, now only jeered.

The townsfolk chuckled, a mischievous grin, Turd Burglar's heart, a twist within.

The glittery prank, a mirror so clear, Turd Burglar tasted his own medicine, of shame & fear.

Remorse filled his eyes, a genuine regret, for the first time, Turd Burglar, couldn't forget

Turd Burglar pondered, a moment so rare, Perhaps a change, a turn of affairs.

The townsfolk watched, with
skeptical eyes,
Could a Turd Burglar truly be wise?

A community puzzled, a Turd Burglar's twist, From mischief to goodness, they couldn't resist.

He painted smiles on faces once sad, Turd Burglar turned them to joyful and glad.

Toilet humor transformed into laughter so sweet, The town found a new hero out on the street

No longer a prankster, but a friend so true, Turd Burglar's heart was happy, through & through.

Through alleys and streets, his legend did grow, From Turd Burglar, to kindness hero.

In the end, a lesson held dear,
Change is possible, and good can
appear.

Turd Burglar's tale, now a town's treasure, From pranks to kindness, a delightful measure.

The End

Made in United States
Orlando, FL
25 November 2024

54429819R00030